Barn Sneeze

Barn Sneeze

Karen B. Winnick

Boyds Mills Press

For Gary, Adam, Alex, Matt, and Mimi, with love
—K. W.

Published by Caroline House
Boyds Mills Press, Inc.
A Highlights Company
815 Church Street
Honesdale, Pennsylvania 18431
Printed in China

U.S. Cataloging-in-Publication Data
   (Library of Congress Standards)

Winnick, Karen B.
     Barn sneeze / written and illustrated by Karen B. Winnick. —1st
ed.
  [32]p. : col. ill. ; cm.
Summary: None of the animals in Sue's barn can stop sneezing.
  ISBN 1-56397-948-9
     1. Domestic animals — Fiction.   2. I. Title.
   [E]   21   2002   CIP   AC
00-102347

First edition, 2002
The text of this book is set in 28-point Gill Sans Bold.

10 9 8 7 6 5 4 3 2 1

The wind went *whoo-whoo*.

Cow sneezed,
"Moo-CHOO. Moo-CHOO."

The hay blew.

"Quack-CHOO," went Duck.
"Quack-CHOO. Quack-CHOO."

He flapped his wings
and up he flew.

Pig awoke.
"Oink-CHOO. Oink-CHOO."

She tripped and fell
on Horse's shoe.

"Neigh-CHOO," sneezed Horse. "Neigh-CHOO. Neigh-CHOO."

Mouse ran out.

He sneezed, too!

Sheep jumped up.
"Baa-CHOO. Baa-CHOO."

She tipped Hen's nest.

"Cluck-CHOO.
Cluck-CHOO."

Hen's one egg rolled . . .

and rolled . . .   and rolled . . .

Rooster crowed,

"Cock-a-doodle-CHOO!"

He woke up Sue.

"Moo." "Squeak." "Neigh." "Peep." "Cluck." "Oink." "Quack." "Baa."

"Cock-a-doodle-doo."

"Aah-CHOO," sneezed Sue.
"Aah-CHOO. Aah-CHOO!"